The Wise Doll

To our mothers

A Red Fox Book

Published by Random House Children's Books
20 Vauxhall Bridge Road, London SW1V 2SA
A division of The Random House Group Ltd
London Melbourne Sydney Auckland
Johannesburg and agencies throughout the world

1 3 5 7 9 10 8 6 4 2

First published in Great Britain by Andersen Press Ltd 1997

Red Fox edition 2000

Printed in Hong Kong

THE RANDOM HOUSE GROUP Limited Reg. No. 954009
www.randomhouse.co.uk

ISBN 0 09 940286 6

The Wise Doll

A traditional tale
retold by Hiawyn Oram
and illustrated by Ruth Brown

RED FOX

ONCE there was a witch called Baba Yaga.
"You are truly terrifying," her trusted Toads told her.
"I should hope so too," said Baba Yaga.
"That's what I'm here for."

One day she looked into her Many-Ways
Mirror and saw what she saw: the Too Nice
Child, the Horrid Child and the Very Horrid Child.

"And I can see which one of them will be
visiting me in the near future," she cackled.

And even as she cackled, Horrid and Very-Horrid
began pushing Too-Nice out. "We don't want you around.
Go away. You're too nice. You can't play with us."

"I know you don't like me," said Too-Nice. "But I can't always
be alone. What shall I do?"

"Go into the forest," said Horrid.

"Visit Baba Yaga," said Very-Horrid. "Bring us back
one of her Toads in a jewelled jacket and diamond collar.
If you do that, we might let you join us."

That night Too-Nice spoke to the Doll her mother
had given her before she died.

"Now what?" she said. "It's unbearable to stay
and it's unbearable to go."

"No one can stay and go at the same time," said
the Doll. "So put me in your pocket, listen to my
advice whenever I have any and let's set out."

So off Too-Nice went with the Doll deep in
her pocket. And, deep in the forest, Baba Yaga
saw her coming.

She pulled her nose down and her chin up until
they met in a terrifying crescent. She called Broom,
Cauldron and all her Toads to her side
and told House to unfold its scaly chicken legs
and take them to meet the advancing child.

When Too-Nice saw the House running towards
her and Baba Yaga peering out of a chimney top,
her legs turned to jelly.

"I can't do this," she said.

"Yes you can," said the Doll from her pocket.

"Just go up and knock and all will be well."
So Too-Nice went up to the House.

"And what do you want?"
squawked Baba Yaga . . .
"Never mind," she sneered.
"Nothing is for nothing. You
want something, you work
for it."

Then Baba Yaga waved at a
mountain of washing-up and a
hill of dirty laundry. "Do it by
morning or Cauldron will
cook you."

Immediately Too-Nice got
down to scrubbing and washing
and ironing, but as midnight
passed she began to tremble.

"I'm cooked," she said to the Doll. "I can't do it."

"Yes you can," said the Doll from her pocket. "You could do it in your sleep. In fact, sleep now and all will be well."

So Too-Nice curled up by the fire and the Doll did the work.

In the morning when the household woke, Baba Yaga was impressed but she didn't show it. She waved at a mountain of dirt in the yard.

"In that dirt," she wheezed, "is an equal amount of poppy seeds. Separate them by this evening or my Toads will taste you."

Immediately Too-Nice got down to work. But as the sun started to drop in the sky, she began to quiver and quake.

"I'm titbits for Toads," she quivered. "I can't do this. Not in one day. Not in a thousand days."

"Yes you can," said the Doll in her pocket. "You can do it with your eyes closed and your hands tied. In fact, shut your eyes for a while, and you'll see, all will be well."

So Too-Nice sat down in the shade and shut her eyes and the Doll did the work.

When the household returned from the forest, Baba Yaga was impressed but she didn't show it. She waved Too-Nice towards the larder.

"In there is a mountain of food. Lay it out for our supper, then join us at the table."

And when the food was laid and they were all at the table, Baby Yaga's eyes glowed like hot coals.

"Now answer me correctly, or you will be my first course. What was it you came here for?"

Immediately Too-Nice opened her mouth to say *Just one of your Toads.*

But she felt the Doll jumping up and down in her pocket and listened to what it meant.

And as Baba Yaga's eyes grew hotter, Too-Nice grew calmer and she answered:

"To get a good scare, of course, because *that's what you're for.*"

And this time Baba Yaga showed she was
impressed. She leapt onto the table and danced
with Broom, Cauldron and Toads in turn.

"That's the right answer, Little Wise One Beyond
Your Years! How did you come to be so wise and
pass all my tests?"

"Hmm," said Too-Nice feeling the Doll in her
pocket. "By a gift from my mother."

"Well, gifts beget gifts!" cackled Baba Yaga.

Then she presented Too-Nice with one of
her Toads – in a pearl-encrusted jacket, a
diamond collar and a long emerald lead.
     And when Too-Nice led the Toad back to Horrid
and Very-Horrid, the Toad wasted no time.
     One! Two! He gobbled them up ...

...and quietly hopped back to the forest.

While Too-Nice, not surprisingly after all she'd been through, stopped being too nice and became ...well ... Just About Right.

Some bestselling Red Fox picture books

THE BIG ALFIE AND ANNIE ROSE STORYBOOK
by Shirley Hughes
OLD BEAR
by Jane Hissey
OI! GET OFF OUR TRAIN
by John Burningham
DON'T DO THAT!
by Tony Ross
NOT NOW, BERNARD
by David McKee
ALL JOIN IN
by Quentin Blake
THE WHALES' SONG
by Gary Blythe and Dyan Sheldon
JESUS' CHRISTMAS PARTY
by Nicholas Allan
THE PATCHWORK CAT
by Nicola Bayley and William Mayne
WILLY AND HUGH
by Anthony Browne
THE WINTER HEDGEHOG
by Ann and Reg Cartwright
A DARK, DARK TALE
by Ruth Brown
HARRY, THE DIRTY DOG
by Gene Zion and Margaret Bloy Graham
DR XARGLE'S BOOK OF EARTHLETS
by Jeanne Willis and Tony Ross
WHERE'S THE BABY?
by Pat Hutchins